MY FIRST
I Can Read Book®

Biscuit Finds a Friend

story by ALYSSA SATIN CAPUCILLI
pictures by PAT SCHORIES

HarperCollins*Publishers*

HarperCollins®, 🐾®, and I Can Read Book®
are trademarks of HarperCollins Publishers Inc.

Biscuit Finds a Friend
Text copyright © 1997 by Alyssa Satin Capucilli
Illustrations copyright © 1997 by Pat Schories
Printed in the U.S.A. All rights reserved.

Library of Congress Cataloging-in-Publication Data
Capucilli, Alyssa.
   Biscuit finds a friend / story by Alyssa Satin Capucilli ;
pictures by Pat Schories.
        p.   cm. — (A my first I can read book)
Summary: A puppy helps a little duck find its way home to the pond.
   ISBN 0-06-027412-3. — ISBN 0-06-027413-1 (lib. bdg.)
   [1. Dogs—Fiction.   2. Ducks—Fiction.]   I. Schories, Pat, ill.   II. Title.
III. Series.
PZ7.C179Bis   1997   96-18368
[E]—dc20   CIP
                                                                  AC

5   6   7   8   9   10
❖

For two very special friends,
Margaret Jean O'Connor and Willie Hornick.

Woof! Woof!

What has Biscuit found?

Is it a ball?

Woof!

Is it a bone?

Woof!

Quack!

It is a little duck.

The little duck is lost.

Woof! Woof!

We will bring
the little duck
back to the pond.

Woof! Woof!

Here, little duck.

Here is the pond.

Here are your mother
and your father.
Quack!

Here are your brothers
and your sisters.
Quack! Quack!

The ducks say thank you.
Thank you for finding
the little duck.

Quack!
The little duck
wants to play.

Quack!

Woof!

Quack!

Woof!

Splash!

Biscuit fell into the pond!

Silly Biscuit.

You are all wet!

Woof!

Oh no, Biscuit.

Not a big shake!

Woof!

Time to go home, Biscuit.

Quack! Quack!

Say good-bye, Biscuit.

Woof! Woof!

Good-bye, little duck.

Biscuit has found
a new friend.

Crazy About CLOUDS

by Rena Korb
illustrations by Brandon Reibeling

Content Consultant:
Raymond Hozalski, Ph.D. • Associate Professor of Environmental Engineering • University of Minnesota

visit us at www.abdopublishing.com

Published by Magic Wagon, a division of the ABDO Publishing Group, 8000 West 78th Street, Edina, Minnesota, 55439. Copyright © 2008 by Abdo Consulting Group, Inc. International copyrights reserved in all countries. All rights reserved. No part of this book may be reproduced in any form without written permission from the publisher. Looking Glass Library™ is a trademark and logo of Magic Wagon.

Printed in the United States.

Text by Rena Korb
Illustrations by Brandon Reibeling
Edited by Nadia Higgins
Interior layout and design by Ryan Haugen
Cover design by Brandon Reibeling

Library of Congress Cataloging-in-Publication Data

Korb, Rena B.
Crazy about clouds / Rena Korb ; illustrated by Brandon Reibeling, content consultant, Raymond Hozalski, Ph.D.
    p. cm. — (Science rocks!)
 ISBN 978-1-60270-037-6
 1. Clouds—Juvenile literature. I. Reibeling, Brandon, ill. II. Title.
 QC921.35.K67 2007
 551.57'6—dc22
                    2007006407

Table of Contents

Cloud Shapes

Look up at the sky. Do you see any clouds today?

Look! There's one shaped like a fluffy, white bunny. A dark gray one floats by like a jellyfish.

Tiny, Floating Drops

The drops in a cloud are very, very small.
Most are smaller than the point of a pin.

Clouds look different. But they are all made of the same stuff—water.

Clouds form when tiny drops of water gather in the sky. Tiny chunks of ice make up clouds, too.

The tiny drops of water come together.
They form heavier and heavier drops.
Sometimes, the drops get too heavy to float.

Splat! Rain pours from the clouds.
Or you might see drizzle, mist, or snow.

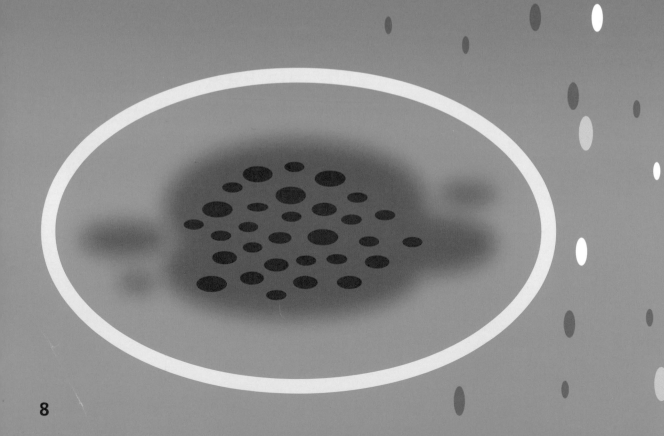

Clouds may look light and fluffy.
But even the water in a small cloud weighs more than 500 tons.
That's about as heavy as 100 elephants!

9

Changing Clouds

Watch a cloud closely.
You will see it change before your very eyes.

Clouds can change shapes and sizes.
They can look bright white or dark gray.
Have you ever seen pink clouds at sunset?

11

Clouds dip and dance as the wind pushes them across the sky.

Some clouds travel as fast as race cars!

A cloud can speed along at 100 miles per hour (160 km/h).

High Clouds, Low Clouds

Scientists group clouds by where they are seen in the sky. High clouds sail with the jumbo jets. Birds fly through low clouds.

Other clouds float in the middle, and some move up and down.

Have you ever walked by a lake on a cool morning? The fog can be very thick. You can barely see the road ahead of you!

Fog is actually a cloud that creeps along the ground.

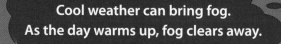

Cool weather can bring fog.
As the day warms up, fog clears away.

Types of Clouds

Scientists also group clouds by how they look. Let's explore a few clouds.

Stratus clouds look like a gray blanket over the sky. They often gather in cool weather. These clouds mean rain may soon be falling.

18

Have you ever seen bright cotton balls in the sky? These are cumulus clouds.

They mostly drift along on a fine, sunny day.

Very high above your head float cirrus clouds. Their long tails curve through the sky.

When you see these clouds, the weather might soon change.

Run for cover!

Dark cumulonimbus clouds are gathering.
These clouds cause powerful storms.

Cumulonimbus clouds usually only stay in the sky for about an hour. As they break open, they can let out millions of buckets of water.

Study the Clouds

Will it rain? Is a snowstorm coming? Clouds give clues about what the weather will be like.

Scientists study clouds to tell what kind of day you'll have tomorrow.

27

You can study the clouds, too. What types of clouds do you see? Can you guess the weather ahead?

No matter what, you are sure to find many wonderful shapes drifting in the sky.

Activity

Make Fog

What you need:

A glass jar

Hot water

A strainer or a cloth towel and a rubber band

Ice cubes

What to do:

1. Have an adult help you fill the jar with the hot water.

2. After about a minute, or when the jar has become hot, pour out most of the water, leaving about 1 inch (about 2½ centimeters) inside of it.

3. Place the strainer or stretch the cloth on top of the jar. If using cloth, fasten it to the mouth of the jar with the rubber band.

4. Place three or four ice cubes in the strainer or on the cloth.

5. Watch the jar and see what happens!

Fun Facts

Basic cloud types	What the cloud looks like	Fun fact	How high the cloud is in the sky
Stratus	Layers and sheets	Clouds may cover the sky and block out the sun and moon.	Low
Cumulus	Puffy and white	Clouds may appear alone or in a group that shows blue sky between them.	High or low
Cirrus	Thin and feathery	Clouds are made entirely of tiny pieces of ice.	High
Cumulonimbus	Tall and gray	Clouds bring bad storms — even tornadoes.	High or low

Glossary

cirrus (SIHR-uhs) cloud—a high cloud that forms thin, white bands.

cloud—a group of tiny drops of water or pieces of ice hanging in the air.

cumulonimbus (KYOO-myuh-luh-NIHM-bus) cloud—a cloud that can rise to great heights and bring storms.

cumulus (KYOO-myuh-luhs) cloud—a cloud that is found at all heights in the sky and forms white puffs.

stratus cloud—a type of low cloud that usually forms gray layers.

On the Web

To learn more about clouds, visit ABDO Publishing Company on the World Wide Web at **www.abdopublishing.com**. Web sites about clouds are featured on our Book Links page. These links are routinely monitored and updated to provide the most current information available.

Index